A Ladybird Book
Series 740

*The story of Ali Baba is taken from a collection
of stories called 'The Thousand and One Nights'.
These stories are based on ancient Persian, Arabian
and Indian tales handed down by word of mouth
for hundreds of years. They first appeared in their
present form, in Arabic, in 1450. The tales are
linked together by the story of Sheherazade.*

*Sheherazade was the wife of the Sultan and had
been condemned to death for her wickedness.
She managed to put off her execution by telling
one of the stories to her sister each night, in the
presence of the Sultan. Being a very clever woman,
as well as a talented storyteller, Sheherazade
always left the most exciting part of the story until
the following night. The Sultan could not bear to
miss the end of each story, and kept on putting off
the execution. For a thousand and one nights
Sheherazade kept the Sultan spellbound with the
stories. He eventually realised that he had been
wrong and forgave Sheherazade.*

*The stories are just as spellbinding today as they
were in those far-off days, and are here presented
in simple text so that younger readers can enjoy
them.*

ALI BABA
and the forty thieves

retold by Marie Stuart

with illustrations by
Robert Ayton

Publishers: Ladybird Books Ltd . Loughborough
© Ladybird Books Ltd 1975
Printed in England

ALI BABA AND THE FORTY THIEVES

Once there were two boys who were brothers. The older one was called Cassim. The other was Ali Baba. When they grew up, Cassim married a woman who was rich.

Ali Baba married a woman who had no money at all, so they had to live in a very small house and never had nice things to eat and drink.

Ali Baba went out every day to cut down trees for firewood. He used to take the wood home on the backs of his three little donkeys. Then he went round the streets with it. Some of the women came out of their houses to buy the wood from him.

This was how he made his living. It was not a very good living and he never had much money to take home to his wife and son.

One day, when he was at work in the woods, he saw some men coming along on horse-back. He did not like the look of them so he said to his donkeys,

"I don't want these men to see me. They may take my wood. You go off so that they will not see you and I will climb up into this tree. I will call you when they have gone."

Up into the tree he went and on came the men. Then the first man said: "Stop! The place is over there!"

All the men jumped from their horses and Ali Baba saw that every horse had a big sack on its back. The men lifted these sacks off the horses' backs and put them on their own backs.

Then the horses were led away and the men walked up to a big rock that was near Ali Baba's tree.

Ali Baba counted the men as they stood nearby. There were forty of them.

Standing in front of the big rock, one of the men called,

"Open Sesame!"

Ali Baba saw a door in the rock open! The man went in and all the others went in after him. No sooner had the last one got in than the door closed again.

"I wish I could get down now and run off home," said Ali Baba, "but they might come out again soon and see me."

So he still sat in the tree. He wondered why he had never seen the door in the rock before! Who had opened it? Was it the entrance to a cave?

And why were the men taking those sacks into it? They were such big sacks – what was in them? Could it be money? Were the men robbers? If so, it would be dangerous to climb down. But what a long time they were!

At last the men came out, and they did not have any sacks with them. When all of them were out, the head man called,

"Close Sesame!"

The door in the rock closed. Then they went to their horses, jumped on their backs and were off and away!

Ali Baba came down from the tree as fast as he could. He went to the rock and called, "Open Sesame!" just as the man had done. At once the door opened and Ali Baba looked into a cave. In it there were not only the sacks which the robbers had left, but many other things – gold, silver, jewels and silks.

There was no time to be lost. If the men came back and found him they would kill him. So he went in quickly to have a good look around.

All of the sacks left by the men were full of money!

He soon pulled the biggest sacks of money up to the door. It had closed after him when he went in, but when he called, "Open Sesame!" it opened at once to let him go out.

Then he said, "Close Sesame!" and it closed.

It did not take him long to find his three donkeys. He put the sacks on their backs with some wood on top, so that no one would know the sacks were there. Then he went home.

His wife did not know what to think when she saw all the money in the sacks. He told her where he had found it but said she must not tell anyone.

"Where will you keep it?" she asked.

"I will dig a pit and put it there," he said.

"First let me see how much there is," she said as she put her hand into one of the sacks. She picked up a handful of coins and let them run through her fingers.

Ali Baba's wife started to count the golden coins,

"One, two, three, four, five, six . . ."

"Stop! It will take too long," said Ali Baba. "You will never count them all. There are so many."

"You dig the pit, and I will go to Cassim's house and ask him to let us have a box to put them in," said his wife. "I want to know how much there is."

"Don't tell them why you want it," said Ali Baba, as she went away.

Cassim was not at home. He was at his shop, but his wife was in the house.

"What do you want a box for?" she asked.

"To put some flour in," replied Ali Baba's wife. "And could you let me have a cup as well? I want to see how much we have."

"Yes, I will go and get one for you. But you must bring it back after you have used it," said Cassim's wife.

As she went to get the cup she thought,
"How can Ali Baba's wife have so much
flour? They have very little money to buy any.
I must find out what she is up to. I know
what to do!"

She put some wax on the bottom of the cup
where it could not be seen. Ali Baba's wife
hurried home as fast as she could with the
box and cup.

"I will see how much money it takes to fill
this cup," she said. "Then we can see how
many cups will fill the box. That way, we
can find out how much money we have."

They found forty cups of money would
go into the box, and they could fill the box
three times from one sack. But they had
three sacks! What a lot of money! And all
gold! How pleased they were.

"Now I must take the cup back," said
Ali Baba's wife.

She did not know that a gold coin was stuck to the wax on the bottom of the cup. Cassim's wife soon found it, and when her husband came home from his shop she said,

"Have you any money?"

"No," said Cassim. "I did not sell much today."

"Ali Baba has some," said his wife.

"What are you saying, woman?" said
Cassim. "You know Ali Baba has no money."

"Aha! He has more than you have," said
his wife. "He has so much gold that he keeps
it in a big box."

Then she told Cassim how she had found
this out. Cassim was not at all pleased and
went to Ali Baba's house to ask him where he
had got the gold.

"How do you know that I have some money?" said Ali Baba.

When Cassim told him how his wife had found out, Ali Baba said,

"All right, I will tell you."

But Cassim was greedy. He did not want to have less money than Ali Baba. So he said,

"You must take me to the place where the gold is. If you don't, I will go to the police and tell them that you are a robber."

Then Ali Baba said, "I will tell you how to find your way to the cave. When you get to the place you will see a tree with a big rock close by. Then you just say,

'Open Sesame!' and a door will open.

When you come out say,

'Close Sesame!' This is all you have to do."

Next day as soon as the sun was up, Cassim went off on his horse. He took eight more horses with him to carry as much money as possible away from the cave. He soon found the right place and the door in the rock.

"Open Sesame!" he called and the door opened. Into the cave he went and the door closed after him. He looked round at all the sacks of gold and jewels. Which should he take? He pulled the biggest ones to the door.

"I don't think I can take any more this time," he said, when he had eight of them. "Now I must get away as fast as I can. I don't want those robbers to find me here."

But he was thinking so much about what was in the sacks that he forgot how to open the door.

He said, "Open Wheat!" not "Open Sesame!" so the door stayed closed.

Then he said : "Open Corn !" But that was not right. "Open Oats !" Nothing happened !

He gave the door a push. Then he pulled, but it would not open. He tried and tried, but he just could not think of the right word to make the door open.

He was still there when the robbers came
to put more sacks in the cave. They saw
Cassim's horses and said to one another,

"Someone must have found out how to get
in. Don't let him get away!"

Then the head man called, "Open Sesame!"

As the door opened Cassim ran out. They
attacked him and left him in the cave, thinking
he was dead.

That night, Cassim's wife went to Ali Baba and said,

"Cassim has not come back. Please try to find him." So Ali Baba went to the cave and found his brother there, nearly dead. He put him on the donkey's back and took him home.

"We must not let anyone know about this," Ali Baba said.

"We must tell people that Cassim is not well. My wife and I will come to your house to help look after him. But he is hurt so badly that we must get some help."

Morgiana, the girl who worked for Cassim's wife said, "I know someone who can help. He is a wise old shoemaker who has made many sick people better. I shall need some money to pay him however."

Next morning, before the sun was up, and when no one was about in the streets, Morgiana went to the old man's shop. He always started work early.

Morgiana said, "Will you come to our house. Someone is very ill. I will give you this money if you will help us."

"Where is your house?" said the old man.

"I cannot tell you," said Morgiana. "You must not see where it is. So close your eyes and keep them closed all the time I am taking you there."

She led him to Cassim's house and up to his bedroom. Then she said, "You may open your eyes now. Can you do anything to save this man's life?"

The wise old man looked at Cassim. He shook his head and said, "This man is very ill, but I will do my best."

The old man bandaged Cassim's wounds, made him a special drink and watched over him for many hours. Then he said, "I can do no more to help this man!"

Then Morgiana said to him, "Thank you for all you have done. Now I will take you back to your shop, but do not tell anyone that you have been here."

The old man closed his eyes and Morgiana took him back to his shop. Two days later Cassim died. Morgiana ran into the street calling, "My master is dead! My master is dead!"

The women came out of their houses to see who was calling. They also saw Cassim's wife at the bedroom window, crying. Next day, Cassim's body was taken outside the city and buried.

After that, Ali Baba and his wife went to live with Cassim's wife in her house, and Ali Baba's son went to work in Cassim's shop.

Three or four days later, the robbers went back to the cave. When they opened the door in the rock they saw that Cassim was no longer there.

"Someone must have taken him away," they said. "One of us must go and find out who it is because whoever did it must know about our cave."

"I will go," said one of the men.

Off he went. Next morning, he came to the street where the old man had his shop. He was sitting at his door with a shoe in his hand.

"Do many people come to you for shoes old man?" said the robber.

"Yes," said the old man, "And they come for other things too. Why only the other day I was asked to try to save the life of a man who had been stabbed and was nearly dead. But it was too late – I could not do much for him."

"What!" said the robber. "Take me to the house where you went and I will give you this bag of gold."

"I don't know where the house is," replied the old man, "because I had to keep my eyes closed all the way. A girl took me."

"Then see if you can find it with your eyes closed," said the robber. "You must know if you went to the right or left, and whether it was a little way or a long way. Come on, give me your hand and close your eyes."

They set off like this and came to a stop at Cassim's house.

"I think this is the right place," said the old man.

The robber made a white cross on the door. Then he took the old man back to his shop, gave him the bag of gold and went away.

When Morgiana went out shopping, she
saw the white cross on their door.

"Who put this there?" she wondered. "It
could have been the children, but I don't
think so. I don't like this. Why is it only on
our house and not on the others?" So she
made some more white crosses on the doors
of the other houses. Then she went on
to do her shopping.

By this time the robber had gone back to the cave.

"I have found the house where the man lives," he said to the others. "Come with me and I will take you to it."

But when they got there he found so many houses with a white cross on the door that he could not tell which was the right one. There was nothing they could do but go back to the cave again.

Then another man said, "Let me try."

So the next day the old man went with him as he did with the first man. When they found the house, a red cross was marked on the door by the robber.

"All the others have a white cross," he said. "This will be the only one with a red cross."

Morgiana saw the red cross when she came back from the shops. So she put some red crosses on the doors of other houses, just as she had done with the white crosses before. When the robbers came again they still could not tell which was the right house.

"This will not do!" said the robber chief. "I must go and find the house myself!"

So he went and found the old man who took him to the house as he had done with the other two men. The head man did not put a cross on it. He had a good hard look at it and went away.

"I must think what to do next," he said to the robbers when he got back. Next day he said,

"I have it!" You must go and buy some big jars – the kind they use for oil. But I want oil in only one of them. The others must have nothing in them.

"Why?" said one of the robbers.

"Because you are going to hide in the jars when you have put them on the horses' backs. I shall take the horses to Ali Baba's house. I shall tell him I have come a long way, and I shall ask him to let me sleep at his house for the night."

"What about us?" said the men.

"You will have to stop in the jars. They are so big there will be plenty of room in them for you. When the time comes I shall tell you what to do."

Things went just as the robber chief had hoped. Ali Baba agreed that he could stay for the night.

Ali Baba helped him to take the jars down from the horses' backs. Then he said, "Come in now and have a good dinner."

After the robber had eaten and drunk all he could, he said, "I must go now and give the horses some water."

While he was in the stable, he went to each jar and spoke to the man who was in it.

"When I make a call like a bird from my window," he said, "you must get out of your jars. I shall come down and tell you what to do." Then he went back into the house.

When Morgiana went to make up the fire
for the night, her lamp went out and she
could not see what she was doing.

"I must buy some more oil in the morning,"
she said, "but tonight I shall take some from
one of those jars."

She went to the first jar and the man who
was in it, thinking she was the robber chief,
said, "Is it time?"

This made her jump, but she quickly
replied in a deep voice,

"Not now. Soon . . ."

She went to the next jar and the next.
Every time the man who was in it said, "Is it
time?" And Morgiana replied, "Not now.
Soon!"

The last jar had oil in it and she put some
in her lamp. Taking some more oil, she boiled it
and tipped some of the boiling oil into each of
the jars. And that was the end of the robbers!

When the robber chief came down in the
night he found his men all dead. So he
jumped on his horse and quickly rode away.

Next morning Morgiana told Ali Baba what
had happened and about the crosses on the
door. He thanked her and said he would
never forget what she had done.

Then he asked some of his men to dig a big
hole in the woods. That night they put the
dead robbers in it.

The robber chief was now alone. So he said, "I shall buy a shop. In it I shall put the silks and jewels that are in the cave. If I sell them I can make a good living."

He did so and everyone said what a good shop it was.

One day, Ali Baba's son met the robber chief. Their shops were near to one another. He asked the robber to come home with him for a meal.

Ali Baba did not remember what the robber chief looked like, but when Morgiana saw him she thought, ''That man has been here before. He means to do something bad. I must stop him.''

So she said to Ali Baba,

''When dinner is over, shall I come in and dance for you?'' Ali Baba said that she could, and after the meal was finished Morgiana came into the room and began to dance.

When she had finished her dance, Morgiana went round the room holding out a cup for them to put money into. Ali Baba gave her some and so did his son. Then she came to the robber chief. As he put some money in the cup, she saw that he had a knife hidden in his clothes.

Before the robber chief could stop her,
she snatched the knife and killed him with it.

"What have you done ?" cried Ali Baba,
jumping up.

"If I had not done that," replied Morgiana,
"he would have killed you. He is the robber
chief who came here with the jars of oil."

Ali Baba saw that Morgiana was right.

"You are a good girl," he said. "I am so pleased with you that I shall be happy if you will marry my son."

So Morgiana and Ali Baba's son were married. When they needed money, they went to the cave and used the robber's treasure. But they made sure that most of it was given to the poor. So everything ended well for everyone but the robbers!